SNOWFLAKE, ANOTHER GREYHOUND'S STORY

By Ginny Anne Folkman

Illustrations by Chrysa Neas

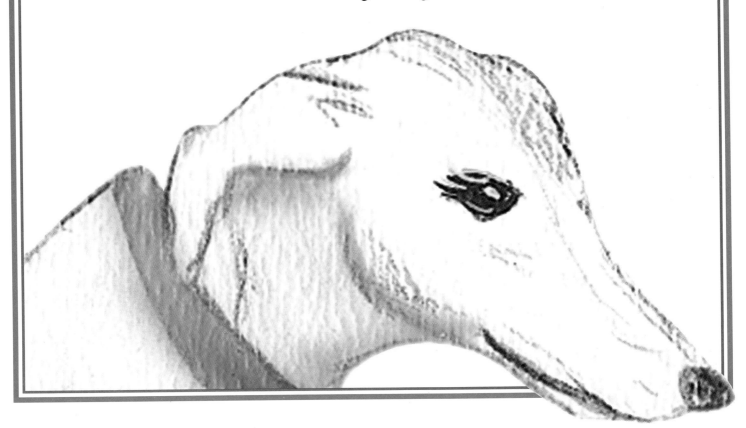

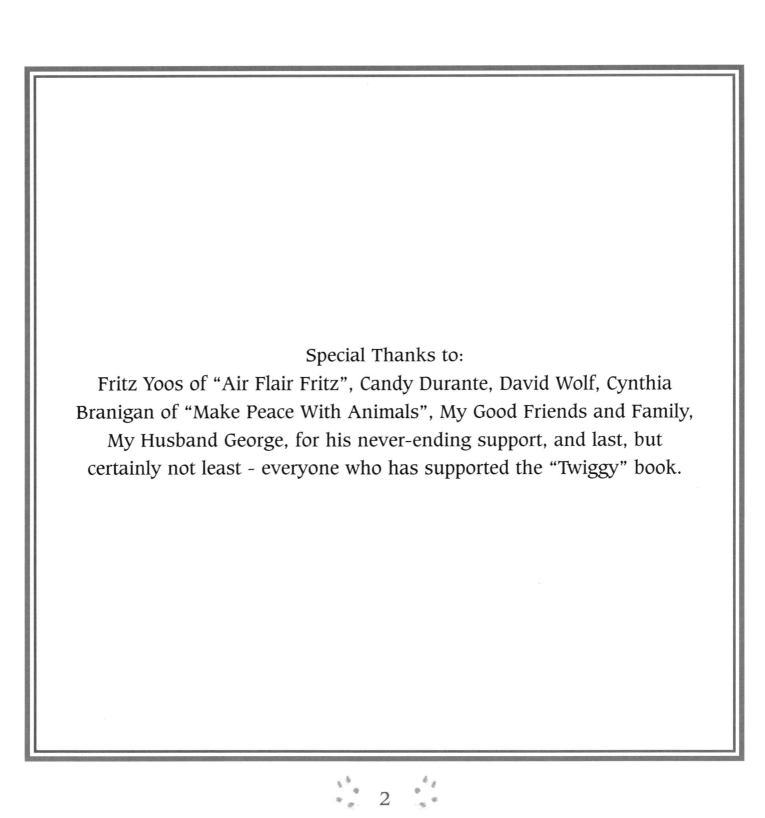

Special Thanks to:
Fritz Yoos of "Air Flair Fritz", Candy Durante, David Wolf, Cynthia Branigan of "Make Peace With Animals", My Good Friends and Family, My Husband George, for his never-ending support, and last, but certainly not least - everyone who has supported the "Twiggy" book.

PREFACE

Greyhounds are the oldest breed of dog, dating back to ancient Egypt. During these ancient times, they were only kept as pets by Pharaohs, Kings, Nobles and other wealthy members of society. Now, thousands of years later, these beautiful creatures of speed and elegance are being sold off into a form of slavery called Greyhound Racing. Even though some are treated well, most racing Greyhounds spend the majority of their lives in caged captivity.

However, no matter how they are treated while they are actively racing, they all face the same two roads of life when their racing careers are over. One road leads to a happy life of comfort, while the other road leads to a very sad end for such a fine animal with such a noble heritage.

Since the printing of the book ***"TWIGGY, STORY OF A GREYHOUND"*** in 1995, thousands of Greyhounds have found their way down the first road and have become wonderful pets to loving families. Unfortunately, too many Greyhounds still have to take the other road in life. A road from which there is no return. This is another Greyhound's story and her race for life.

Chapter 1:
BORN TO RUN

"**H**ere comes another one! It's another white one!! And it's a girl!" Jimmy called out to his assistant. "That makes five puppies so far!"

Jimmy is a greyhound breeder in Oklahoma. Over the years he has seen many greyhound puppies born and he seemed to have a fondness for them all. But when they leave his care and training, he has to turn his back to what one day may be a horrible fate. "What would become of this tiny white furry snowball?" He couldn't help but wonder.

"We'll call this one XS Snowflake, and we'll call her brother, the other white puppy, Pure White," Jimmy said.

Snowflake's personality was evident from the day she was born. She was so sweet, timid and polite. She would let her brother and sisters push their way in front of her to drink milk from their mother. When the puppies weren't eating, they were sleeping. Somehow, Snowflake always

got pushed off to the side. But, she didn't seem to mind.

It would be a couple of weeks before Snowflake opened her eyes. But what a set of eyes she would turn out to have! It looked as if her eyes were outlined with black eye liner. When she looked your way, she could melt your heart with those soulful, sweet eyes.

At about eight weeks she and her brother and sisters were weaned from their mother and were able to eat on their own. It was now time to

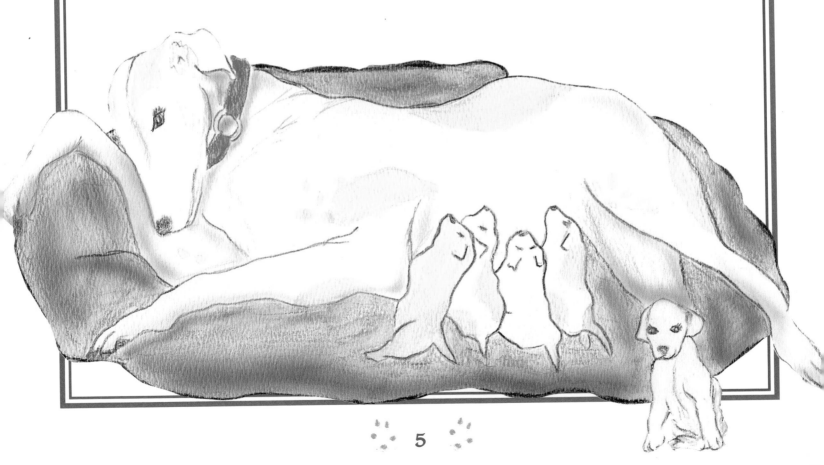

have their ears tattooed. This was done so the dogs could be identified when they left the breeding farm. Since Snowflake was the fifth puppy born in the litter, the letter E and her date of birth were tattooed in her right ear. The serial number of her owner was tattooed in her left ear.

The puppies would now begin to train for their racing career.

Chapter 2:
THE TRAINING

To start their training the puppies would chase a fuzzy ball on the end of a rope that their trainer would pull in front of them. Later on, when the puppies reached about six months old, he would attach a plastic jug to the back end of a slow moving tractor and the puppies would chase after it as it was dragged along the ground.

The next step in their training was to have the puppies chase a lure that looked like a fuzzy rabbit. The lure looked like it was suspended in mid-air because it was supported from a whirligig. The lure spun in a circle and the puppies ran as fast as they could to try and catch it. Their final training would be running on a track similar to the ones they would eventually race on when they reached racing age. The puppies reached racing age when they turned about twenty months old.

Even though Snowflake was shy and timid, she liked to chase the fuzzy lure. She loved playing with her brother and sisters, romping and rolling on the ground. She was very gentle when she played. Her brother, Pure White, was a bit of a bully though. For several months the whole litter of puppies were put together in a narrow, fenced-in run which was the length of a football field. The puppies played and ran back and forth for up to a half hour. This was good exercise and helped to build their muscles. Even at this young age, the puppies competed against each other while running back and forth.

After a day of training, Snowflake would be put in her cage along side all the other dogs in their cages. The cages were like bunk beds, one on top of another, all lined up in a long row. Snowflake would drift off to sleep to the sound of music playing in the background.

There was always music playing so the dogs wouldn't be awakened by outside noises such as other dogs barking or the sound of trucks driving in and out of the kennel grounds. They needed their rest to train and race and the music seemed to have a soothing and calming effect on the greyhounds.

Chapter 3:
A SPECIAL BOND

Snowflake really loved people. She would have liked to spend more time with her trainer, but he was so busy with all the other puppies.

Sometimes Jimmy's children would come to the kennel to play with the puppies. Snowflake loved to sniff and lick them. And if they had ice cream or chocolate on their faces, she would lick and lick until it tickled them. Katie was eleven years old and was the oldest of the children. Melissa was ten and Amber was nine. The three girls looked almost like triplets; all with honey blonde hair and beautiful blue eyes. And then there was Cory. He was the youngest child. He was eight years old, but he didn't look much like his sisters. He had wavy brown hair and big brown eyes. The girls didn't visit the puppies as much as Cory did. They had their own friends, Mallory, Ashley and Emily, to keep them busy. There were tea parties, dolls and many games to play. Cory had his friends too. There was Zakeri, Justin and Tommy. They loved fishing and playing sports after school and they really wanted Cory to go along with them. It wasn't that Cory didn't want to go fishing and play sports, he just loved being with the puppies more. Everyday he would visit them before and after school.

He was especially fond of Snowflake. Sometimes he would sneak extra visits with her when the trainer was busy with the other puppies.

Jimmy didn't want the children to become overly attached to the puppies. After all, this wasn't going to be their permanent home. But Snowflake and Cory formed a special bond. He would bring her extra treats whenever he could. As time passed by he began to think of Snowflake as his dog and she really looked forward to his visits. One day, he finally got up the courage to ask his dad if Snowflake could come to live with them at the house. He even planned to have Snowflake sleep with him in his room.

As Cory was on his way to talk to his dad, he overheard the trainer and his father talking about Snowflake.

"Tomorrow Snowflake will be leaving for Florida," Jimmy said.

"How are you going to tell Cory?" the trainer asked. "He will be very upset. He's here every day. I've seen him sneak in to see her. You know Jimmy, Cory thinks Snowflake is his dog."

"I know! I've tried to explain to him from a young age that this is my job and he knows all the greyhounds would have to leave at racing age. This is exactly what I was afraid of. I'm just going to have to figure out a way to deal with this. Maybe his mother and sisters can help by having a talk with him. I just hope he'll understand someday," Jimmy said as he was walking back towards the house where they lived.

"I'll see you tomorrow," Jimmy said as he waved goodbye to the trainer.

Cory couldn't believe what he was hearing. This couldn't be true. He was sure his father would let him keep Snowflake. Cory ran as fast as he could to the kennel where Snowflake was kept. She was sleeping soundly. He opened the door to her cage and crawled inside with her.

Snowflake was happy to see him but she sensed something was wrong. Cory's eyes filled with tears. As he stroked Snowflake very

gently, his tears fell on her soft, velvet-like fur.

"Why can't you stay with me, Snowflake, and be my dog. Don't they know how much I love you. I'll never love another dog the way I love you. It's just not fair," Cory sobbed.

Snowflake licked the salty tears running down Cory's cheek. She hated to see him so sad. She could feel her heart breaking. Neither of them understood why things had to be this way.

The next day the trainer went to get Snowflake ready for the trip to Orlando, Florida. When he got to Snowflake's cage, he found Cory curled around her. Cory had snuck out in the middle of the night to sleep with Snowflake.

"Cory, do your parents know where you've been all night?" the trainer asked.

"No," Cory said as he wiped his puffy red eyes.

The trainer knew Cory had cried himself to sleep.

"Cory, I know you're upset. I've gotten attached to some of the greyhounds too. They're such loving animals, you can't help but grow fond of them. But you know this is your dad's business."

"I know," Cory said softly, "But Snowflake is so special."

"And I'm sure she feels the same way about you Cory, but you can see why your dad worries about his children becoming too attached to the dogs," the trainer said trying to comfort Cory. "I'm sorry, Cory, you know it's time to get Snowflake loaded in the truck for the trip."

"Can I just have one more minute?" Cory pleaded.

"Sure kid," the trainer said as he turned and walked out.

Cory hugged Snowflake's neck so tightly. He wanted to hug her forever. He leaned over and kissed her softly on the side of her head for the last time. She licked his cheek before he bravely turned to leave.

"I'll always love you Snowflake. I hope you don't forget me. I know I'll never forget you," Cory said as his voice quivered.

As Cory walked to the door of the kennel, Snowflake didn't take her eyes off of him.

The door slowly closed. That was the last time Snowflake would see Cory.

When the trainer returned, Cory was gone. He got Snowflake's collar and leash and walked her to the truck. She looked around desperately for Cory, but she didn't see him anywhere. She was really scared to be leaving him and the only home she knew. Cory had always been there to give her love and affection.

As she curled up in the truck cage, she was not quite sure of what was happening to her. She knew that her brother Pure White and her sisters had already been sent to a race track in another state. Without them and without Cory, she felt so alone.

Chapter 4:
THE MAIDEN RACE

It would take about one and a half days of continuous driving to reach Orlando, Florida. It was hard for Snowflake to sleep in the truck during her trip with the constant bumps in the road and without the familiar music playing in the background. She knew Cory wouldn't be greeting her in the morning before he went to school. And Pure White was no longer only a couple of cages away like he was in their old kennel. That night was like an eternity.

When the truck arrived at the race track, it was midday. Snowflake was escorted to her new kennel and cage. Her maiden race would be in a week. But first, she would have to begin training on the new track to get accustomed to it. When the night of her maiden run finally came, Snowflake was scheduled to be in the first race. While she was running, all she could think of was Cory and her brother and sisters and how much she missed them. It left such an empty feeling in her heart. She didn't do

very well that race. She came in seventh. This was not a good beginning
for a race dog. She thought that maybe if she didn't do well they might
send her back to Oklahoma and she could be with Cory again. But
Snowflake didn't know how the greyhound racing business worked.

She soon learned what happened to those dogs who continued to
lose. They were never seen again. But, she still had five more races to

prove herself a good runner. Day by day her running was improving and she was getting faster and faster; but, winning wasn't everything to her. She felt so sorry for the other dogs; something inside of Snowflake wanted the other dogs to win. She never wanted to see anyone hurt or upset. Some of the dogs were so aggressive they would push her out of the way to win. Sometimes, there were accidents on the track during a race. During one race, her new-found greyhound friend, Ruby Raindrop, broke her leg in a pileup on the track. Ruby Raindrop was never seen again after that race.

Five races later, Snowflake hadn't won any money running the races. She overheard her trainers at the racetrack saying, "XS Snowflake doesn't have what it takes to be a winner. We're going to have to get rid of her soon."

Snowflake began to shake and couldn't stop. Now she knew for sure that she wasn't going to be sent back to Oklahoma.

"What will happen to me now?" she wondered as she was placed into her cage for the night. That night, she had nightmares and whimpered in her sleep. Even the music couldn't calm her.

Chapter 5:
RESCUED IN THE NICK OF TIME

The next morning Snowflake was outside for the morning turnout. She saw a truck drive onto the grounds she had never seen before. It had "National Greyhound Adoption Program" printed on the side.

David Wolf, the founder of the greyhound adoption program, had sent his specially made truck to pick up as many dogs as it could carry before they were destroyed. Snowflake and thirty two others were rescued that day, just in the nick of time. She heard the driver say they were going to Philadelphia, Pennsylvania. As the truck pulled off the grounds, Snowflake wished she was going back to Oklahoma. But she sensed something was different about this truck. She wasn't quite as scared as she had been in the truck on her trip to Florida, but she was still worried about what lay ahead of her. "It smells so clean and I'm laying on thick carpet," she thought. Still, she was so exhausted from worry she slept most of the trip. When the truck arrived in Philadelphia, Snowflake

and the other dogs were taken to the kennel. There were volunteers who would come to the kennel to help out whenever they could. A volunteer named Buff took Snowflake to a bright and cheerful room.

There she had her teeth cleaned and she was given a nice warm bath. As Snowflake was being bathed, she heard the most wonderful sound. From the kennel where all the greyhounds were kept, she could hear all the dogs howling together. To greyhounds, howling is the song of contentment. Snowflake knew she was someplace special and she felt secure. After her bath, she was sprayed with a sweet smelling doggie perfume. She never felt so clean and pretty. Next, she was given a big meal and boy, did she gobble it up! From now on, she was going to be fed twice a day instead of once a day. Then Snowflake was put into a nice, roomy, clean cage with a soft, plush carpet. It wasn't long before she was fast asleep.

Snowflake was in the adoption kennel ten days. The adoption program arranged for a family from another state to adopt Snowflake, but the family changed their mind at the last minute.

David was very disappointed. He realized how sweet and special

Snowflake was. Then he remembered that there was a family who lived nearby. They had already adopted one greyhound and now they wanted to adopt a second greyhound. He made a quick phone call.

The next day, Snowflake heard the door to her kennel open. Who was this family standing in the front of her cage?

It was George, Ginger, Mikie, Linda and a beautiful brindle-colored greyhound named Twiggy.

Linda excitedly said, "She's so beautiful!" They all agreed when they saw Snowflake.

David let Snowflake out of her cage. Immediately, Twiggy trotted over to Snowflake and sniffed her all over. They both wagged their tails.

"I think they like each other," Mikie said.

"Can we take her home today?" Linda and Mikie asked at the same time.

"Sure, the paperwork should only take about an hour, so of course you can take her home today," David replied.

Snowflake walked over to David wagging her tail. She licked his hand which was her way of saying 'thank you for taking such good care of me'. Somehow all of the greyhounds sensed David had saved them from a terrible fate. He was so happy to see another greyhound going to a good home.

While waiting for the paperwork to be finished, the family went shopping at the kennel. You could find everything you needed there. Linda and Mikie picked out a big new bed and a pretty collar for Snowflake. Twiggy wasn't jealous. She already had so many nice things of her own. She was even willing to share her bone with Snowflake. "I'm glad everything worked out," David said. "We will see you at the greyhound picnic in September, I hope," he added. "We'll all be there," George said.

Chapter 6:
A NEW BEGINNING

Linda and Mikie couldn't wait for Snowflake to see her new home.

Snowflake stood up in the car all the way home. She was a bit nervous not knowing where she was going. Then she saw a road sign that said "SUMNEYTOWN 3 MILES".

As they turned onto the long driveway to the house, Snowflake was still nervous, but it was nothing new to Twiggy. She had been back and forth in the car so many times she knew exactly where she was. Twiggy jumped up wagging her tail. But Snowflake was swaying and her long skinny legs were wobbling.

As they pulled up to the big white house, Snowflake couldn't believe what she saw. It was so beautiful. There were so many flowers and bushes blooming. Every color in the rainbow surrounded the house and the walkway to the front door. As Snowflake walked down the pathway,

she stopped to sniff some of the flowers. The smells were so wonderful, even sweeter than the perfume she was sprayed with.

Twiggy knew Snowflake might have a hard time with the front steps since she had never seen steps before. This is because greyhounds are lifted in and out of their cages at the race track. So Twiggy ran ahead to show her what to do. Snowflake appreciated Twiggy's help, but she still

had a hard time with the steps. But it wouldn't be very long before she was racing Twiggy up and down the stairs. Twiggy would be a big help in showing Snowflake the ropes of living in a house with a family.

That night after dinner when everything calmed down, Linda took Twiggy and Snowflake to her room. She put their beds together so Snowflake wouldn't be lonely.

"I hope you will be happy here Snowflake," Linda said as she softly kissed the top of Snowflake's head. Twiggy curled up next to Snowflake and rested her head on Snowflake's back. She sniffed her neck a couple of times and licked her ear very tenderly. As Snowflake was drifting off to sleep, a calmness came over her. There was so much love from Twiggy and her new family. And what a wonderful and warm place to live! She had a comfortable bed to sleep on and plenty of toys and bones. She had the freedom of roaming from room to room and a big back yard in which to run and play. Now she could run for fun and she didn't have to worry about winning. There were so many new things to experience. It wasn't that Snowflake didn't appreciate her new home and family, but she still felt a little tug on her heart when she thought of Cory and the time she spent in Oklahoma. She would always remember the special bond she had with him.

Snowflake couldn't help but think of Cory now without sighing. She slowly closed her eyes. Tomorrow was the first day of a long and happy life.

THE END

GLAMOUR GIRL
SNOWFLAKE

Twiggy lends a paw at a booksigning

Children welcome Snowflake and Twiggy to their school

Ginny, proud owner of Snowflake and Twiggy, poses with her first book

Ginny and the girls at a booksigning

Look out supermodels!...Snowflake and Twiggy were two of many stars in a fashion show held in New York City to benefit

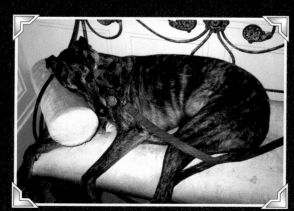

SCRAPBOOK PAGES

Bathing Beauties...
Snowflake and
Twiggy cool off
from the summer
heat by splashing
in their pool

*Relaxing at home
is what
Snowflake and
Twiggy love
the most!*

Snowflake and Twiggy brave the
Blizzard of January 1996

Ginny's husband,
George, stops to take a
rest with Snowflake
and Twiggy - while
Snowflake makes a
new friend with a fluffy
white dog at a benefit
for a new local library

If you would like information on adopting a greyhound, call National Greyhound Adoption at 1-800-348-2517.

If you would like more information about greyhounds, the following books are available at your local library or local book store:

- *Twiggy Story of a Greyhound* by Ginny Anne Folkman Emerald Press ISBN 0-9644470-0-2

- *Adopting the Racing Greyhound* by Cynthia A. Branigan ISBN 0-87605-190-5